Twin
Troubles

Twin Troubles

Susan Beth Pfeffer

Illustrated by
Abby Carter

A Redfeather Book

Henry Holt and Company   *New York*

First edition
Published by Henry Holt and Company, Inc.,
115 West 18th Street, New York, New York 10011.
Published simultaneously in Canada by Fitzhenry & Whiteside Ltd.,
91 Granton Drive, Richmond Hill, Ontario L4B 2N5.

Library of Congress Cataloging-in-Publication Data
Pfeffer, Susan Beth.
    Twin troubles / Susan Beth Pfeffer; illustrated by Abby Carter.
    (A Redfeather book)
    Summary: Eight-year-old Crista has the worst week of her
life, experiencing bad times at school and at home, but when
her twin sister Betsy tries to sympathize by sharing her bad
times it causes a fight.
    ISBN 0-8050-2146-9
    [1. Twins—Fiction. 2. Sisters—Fiction. 3. Family life—
Fiction.] I. Carter, Abby, ill. II. Title. III. Series:
Redfeather books.
PZ7.P44855Tx   1992
[Fic]—dc20   92-5773

Printed in the United States of America
on acid-free paper.∞

10 9 8 7 6 5 4 3 2 1

*To the wonderful people at
the Miracle Mile Bagel Bakery
of Middletown, New York*

Contents

1 · School Troubles   1

2 · Supper Troubles   7

3 · Store Troubles   13

4 · Betsy's Troubles   19

5 · Once-in-a-Lifetime Troubles   25

6 · Homework Troubles   31

7 · Tooth Troubles   37

8 · Digging Up Troubles   43

9 · Twin Troubles   49

School Troubles

"**C**rista, what is five times six?"

Crista Linz had been staring out the window, thinking about her kitten Misty. She and her twin sister, Betsy, had brought their kittens home just the day before. Crista worried that Misty would get lost in her new home, or that Marty, Crista and Betsy's baby brother, might fall on Misty and squoosh her. For every two steps Marty took, he fell once.

"Crista, I asked you what is five times six?"

Crista heard her name and realized the other kids were looking at her. She thought she heard a couple of giggles. "I'm sorry," she said.

"Are you sorry because you weren't listening or

· 1

because you don't know the answer?" her teacher, Mr. Lopez, asked.

"I don't know," Crista said. "I mean both. Either. I mean either."

This time everybody laughed except Crista. Even Mr. Lopez had a smile on his face.

"Are you paying attention now?" he asked.

Crista nodded. She was listening with every part of her ears.

"What is five times six?" Mr. Lopez asked.

"That's easy," Crista said, relieved that the question was one she could answer. "Six times six is thirty-six."

Everyone laughed even harder then, except for Mr. Lopez. Crista looked around for her sister Betsy. Betsy wasn't laughing. She was just shaking her head and mouthing something to Crista.

Crista could usually understand what Betsy was saying even if she couldn't hear her. Their mother sometimes said the twins didn't need words, they knew each other so well. But this time Crista had no idea what Betsy was trying to tell her.

"Look at me, Crista," Mr. Lopez said. "I know you know the answer."

"I just told you the answer," Crista said. "Six times six is thirty-six."

The class really laughed then. Crista hadn't heard them laugh so hard since the clown had been at the school assembly. And that was way back in first grade.

"Betsy, I saw you trying to help Crista out," Mr. Lopez said. "Do you want to tell the whole class the answer, or just your sister?"

"Five times six is thirty," Betsy said. "But Crista was right. Six times six *is* thirty-six."

"Both answers are right," Mr. Lopez said. "Thank you, Betsy."

Betsy smiled at Crista. Crista tried to smile back.

"Crista, what lesson have you learned just now?" Mr. Lopez asked.

Crista wasn't sure. "I should pay more attention to what Betsy's telling me?" she asked.

"Not when she's trying to give you the answers," Mr. Lopez said. "Instead, pay more attention to your lessons. Daydreaming is fine. We all need to do it sometimes, but not during arithmetic."

Betsy raised her hand. "Sometimes I don't pay attention," she said. "Sometimes I daydream just like Crista."

"Betsy and Crista do everything the same," Jane said. Jane was a good friend of both the twins.

"We feel the same too," Betsy said. "When Crista's sad, I'm sad. And she knows what I know, so she knew what six times five was too. Honest, Mr. Lopez."

Mr. Lopez looked at the twins and laughed. "I'm sure she did," he said. "Crista, what's six times four?"

Crista's face turned bright red. "I'm sorry," she said. "I was thinking about how Betsy and I are alike."

"I was too," Betsy said. "Crista and I were having the exact same thought."

"I told you they were the same," Jane said.

"Amazing," Mr. Lopez said. "Class, let's all tell Crista what six times four is."

"Twenty-four," the class all said, except for a couple of kids who said "Twenty-six."

"Very good," Mr. Lopez said. "Are we ready to move on?"

Crista certainly was. Actually, by then, she was ready to move out.

Supper Troubles

"**D**id anything interesting happen in school today?" Crista's father asked that night at supper. The family was sitting around the dining-room table. They always ate together—Mr. and Mrs. Linz, and Crista and Betsy and Marty and their big sister, Grace. Grace was twelve, and sometimes really interesting things happened to her just because she was big.

"I had a science test," Grace said. "I think I did okay on it. And Jennifer Daley puked in the middle of gym class."

"No puking talk at the dinner table," Mrs. Linz said. She always said that when someone wanted to talk about puking.

Marty banged his spoon against the high chair.

Sometimes even if he hadn't puked, his tray looked like he had.

"Did anything else happen in school, Grace?" Mr. Linz asked. "Did you get your spelling test back?"

"I got a ninety," Grace said. "Hardly anyone got a hundred. It's hard to when Mrs. Smith gives a spelling test. She doesn't say the words loud enough. She mumbles, you know. We all try to hear her, but we can't."

"Have any of you told her that?" Mr. Linz asked.

Grace nodded. "We did right after the first spelling test," she said. "And Mrs. Smith said it was good for us. That way we'd really have to listen."

"Ah ah ah ah ah ah ah," Marty said. No one listened to him.

"Chips wants something to eat," Betsy said. Her kitten was named Chips. He was black with a white face. Misty was gray with a white face. Chips was trying to climb up Betsy's leg. "Can I give him something, Mom?"

"Not from your plate," Mrs. Linz said. "If you

do, he'll get into the habit of asking all the time. So will Misty. Cats get fed cat food and people get fed people food. I think you should tell Chips that rule right now."

Betsy helped Chips up her leg. He sat on her lap and purred. "No food," Betsy said. "But I'll pet you."

Chips purred even louder.

"Where's Misty?" Grace asked.

"I don't know," Crista said. She'd played with Misty when they'd gotten home from school, but she hadn't seen her since. Maybe Marty had squooshed her. "Mommy, have you seen Misty?"

"I see her," Betsy said. "She's in the corner there. I think she's hiding from us."

"Why should she hide?" Crista asked.

"Maybe she's seen the way Marty eats," Grace said.

"Misty's more of a watching kind of cat," Mrs. Linz said. "Chips is more of a climbing kind of cat. Just because they're brother and sister doesn't mean they have the same kind of personality."

"Crista and I do," Betsy said. "We're just the same all the time."

"You're twins," Mr. Linz said. "Twins are different from kittens. Besides, you and Crista aren't exactly alike either. Just more alike than most other people."

"We are too exactly alike," Betsy said. "Today in school, when Crista wasn't listening, I wasn't listening either."

"What are you talking about?" Mrs. Linz asked.

Crista wished Betsy hadn't brought it up. "Mr. Lopez asked me a question and I got it wrong," she said. "So he told all of us we shouldn't daydream."

"But the thing was, I was daydreaming too," Betsy said. "Just not as hard as Crista was. So I knew the answer when Mr. Lopez called on me. But I almost wouldn't have."

"How could you almost not know an answer?" Grace asked.

"I almost said thirty-five," Betsy said. "And that would have been even worse than what Crista did. She said thirty-six, when the answer was thirty."

"Why would thirty-five have been worse?" Grace asked. "It's closer to thirty than thirty-six is."

"But we were doing our six tables," Betsy said. "If I'd said thirty-five, then Mr. Lopez would have known I thought we were doing our five tables. I was really thinking about Chips."

"And I was thinking about Misty," Crista said. "We really are exactly alike."

"If you're going to be exactly alike, could you be exactly alike and listen to your teacher?" Mrs. Linz asked. "Instead of being exactly alike about your kittens?"

Crista and Betsy nodded. Marty threw his spoon at Misty, who ran out of the dining room to safety.

"You won't see her again tonight," Grace said.

"That's okay, Crista," Betsy said. "You can play with Chips and me. Right, Chips?"

Chips purred. Crista tried to smile, but she wished she could play with her own kitten instead. Maybe she and Betsy should give Misty and Chips lessons in being more alike.

Store Troubles

"I'm going to the bookstore, Mom," Grace said after school the next day. "Okay?"

"Don't stay too long," Mrs. Linz said. "And don't spend too much."

"I won't," Grace said.

"Can I go with you?" Crista asked.

Grace looked down at her sister. "You won't do anything dumb?" she asked.

"I won't," Crista said. "I promise."

"All right," Grace said.

Crista ran into her room. Betsy was on her bed, playing with Chips and Misty. Misty seemed to be having a great time. "I'm going to the bookstore with Grace," Crista said. "Want to come?"

Betsy shook her head. "I'll stay here with the kittens," she said.

Crista nodded. She opened the little box where she kept money she was saving, and she took out two dollar bills and three quarters and two dimes. That was what the new Jenny Archer book cost in paperback.

"Hurry up!" Grace called. Crista ran out of the room and joined Grace at the door.

"I'm going to buy the new Jenny Archer," Crista told Grace. "She's my favorite."

"Okay," Grace said. "You have enough money?"

Crista nodded happily. She loved reading. She'd already read the book she was going to buy at school, but now she could own her own copy. She'd been saving her money for three weeks to buy the book. She could hardly wait until she got it home.

Betsy liked to read, but not as much as Crista did. That was one way the twins were a little different from each other. Crista wondered if Misty liked to read more than Chips. She giggled.

"No giggling at the bookstore," Grace said. "If

you just stand there giggling, everyone will think you're crazy."

"I'm sorry," Crista said, even though she wasn't. She'd learned a long time ago it made things easier just to say you were sorry to Grace. Grace didn't care if you meant it.

The bookstore was four blocks away. Crista loved living only four blocks from a bookstore. She couldn't wait until she was old enough to walk there by herself. She would have skipped to get there faster, but she didn't think Grace would like that. She didn't feel like saying "I'm sorry" twice in one block, either. So she just walked.

"Don't do anything dumb," Grace said again as they entered the store. "I don't want the world to know what a dumb kid sister I have."

"I won't, I promise," Crista said. Someday she'd probably tell Marty not to do anything dumb. Right now just about everything he did was dumb, but he was a baby, so it looked cute. Crista tried to picture Marty eight years old. All she could see was a baby her own size, wearing an enormous diaper. She giggled loudly.

"No giggling," Grace whispered angrily. "I warned you."

"Sorry," Crista said. It was hard not to giggle at a giant Marty. She coughed instead.

Grace went to the section of the bookstore she was interested in, and Crista walked over to the younger kids' books. There it was, the new Jenny Archer. It looked even better in paperback than it had in hardback. She could hardly wait to own it.

She looked at all the other books for sale. They looked good too, but she knew what she was going to buy. She'd known for three weeks. She carried the book to the counter to pay for it.

"Are you paying for this yourself?" the sales clerk asked.

Crista nodded.

"And you have enough money?" the sales clerk asked.

Crista felt the money in her pocket. She nodded again.

The sales clerk rang up the cost on the cash

register. "That's three dollars and thirteen cents," she said.

"No it isn't," Crista said. "It's two dollars and ninety-five cents." She pointed to the cost of the book. It was right there on the cover. Two dollars and ninety-five cents.

"There's eighteen cents' sales tax," the sales clerk said. "Three dollars and thirteen cents, please."

"I don't have three dollars and thirteen cents," Crista said. "I only have two dollars and ninety-five cents. Do I have to pay sales tax? I'm only eight."

The clerk laughed. "That's really cute, kid," she said. "But eight or eighty, we all have to pay."

Crista looked over at Grace. She didn't dare ask her for the money. Instead she took the book and put it back where she found it. Next week she'd have three dollars and thirteen cents. But it just wasn't fair that she couldn't buy the book she wanted right then and there. And she hated it when she made a mistake and people said it was cute.

Betsy's Troubles

"**D**id you buy anything?" Betsy asked when Crista got home from the store.

Crista shook her head. "I didn't have enough money," she said. "I forgot about sales tax. They laughed at me."

"That's terrible," Betsy said.

Crista felt like crying. She hated being laughed at, and now it had happened twice in two days.

Chips and Misty didn't seem to care about Crista's troubles. They kept chasing each other on Betsy's bed. Sometimes they ran right over Betsy to get to each other. Betsy giggled every time they did that. Crista wished Betsy would stop.

"Did Grace see what happened?" Betsy asked.

"No," Crista said.

"Well, that's good," Betsy said. "The same thing happened to me once. I was with Grace at the store, and I wanted to buy a little teddy bear. It was so cute. Not as cute as Chips, but cute, and I thought I had enough money, so I took it to the counter and said I wanted to buy it. And the clerk asked me to show her all my money, and I did, and I was fifty-five cents short. And the clerk asked me if I knew how to count, and did I know what money was, and it was terrible."

"What did you do?" Crista asked. She wondered what would happen if she picked Misty up and brought her to her bed to play. Betsy picked Chips up all the time, and Chips loved it.

"I asked Grace for the money," Betsy said. "Oh look, Crista."

Crista looked. Misty was trying to catch her own tail, and Chips was running around her. They were going faster and faster. Betsy was laughing really hard, and soon even Crista was laughing. Kittens didn't mind if you laughed at them.

Misty stopped very fast, and Chips fell on top of her. In an instant they were both snoring.

"Maybe we should sleep that way," Betsy said.

"I think it's easier if you have fur," Crista said. "Did Grace give you the money?" She didn't want to tell Betsy she'd been too scared to ask Grace herself.

"No," Betsy said. "She got real mad at me. She said she was never taking me to a store again. She said little kids shouldn't be let into stores, that they should just wait outside while older kids shopped. She said she was sorry she ever had twin sisters and she never ever wanted to see me again. You know. She said Grace stuff."

"Did you say you were sorry?" Crista asked.

"I did not," Betsy said. "I said she was mean and rotten and I stuck my tongue out at her. Like this." Betsy stuck her tongue out at Crista. She looked pretty silly.

"You look like Chips getting ready to give Misty a bath," Crista said.

"I do?" Betsy asked. She hopped off the bed to check herself out in the mirror. "I need more fur," she said, once she'd looked.

"What did Grace do?" Crista asked. She would

never have the nerve to stick her tongue out at Grace in a store.

"She screamed for Mom," Betsy said, getting back on her bed. The kittens kept sleeping. "Mom was with you and Marty. Marty was real little then. Mom told Grace not to scream and me not to bother Grace."

"Did you mind?" Crista asked.

"I minded a lot," Betsy said. "It was terrible. Grace was mad at me and Mom was mad at me and I didn't even get the teddy bear I wanted. It was almost the worst thing that ever happened to me. It was a lot worse than what happened to you today."

"Why?" Crista asked. She figured what had happened to her had been pretty bad.

"Grace didn't get mad at you and Mom didn't get mad at you," Betsy said. "And we only live four blocks from the bookstore. You can go back next week and buy the book. When I went back to buy the teddy bear, it was months later, and they didn't have it anymore. See what I mean."

"I do," Crista said, but she felt like she did when she apologized to Grace and didn't mean it. What happened to Betsy was definitely bad, but Crista didn't see why it was worse than what had happened to her. Nobody had laughed at Betsy. It didn't seem fair that no matter how bad things that happened to Betsy were, things that happened to Crista were just a little bit worse.

•5•

Once-in-a-Lifetime Troubles

C rista sat in her bedroom and looked down at her homework. It was just arithmetic. Usually she had no trouble with her arithmetic homework. But today she couldn't seem to remember any of the answers.

She could hear Betsy and Jane in the living room. They were playing with the kittens. Crista wanted to be there with them, but her mother had told her to finish her homework first.

Six times seven was . . . Crista knew she knew. She knew all her multiplication tables better even than Betsy. So why had Betsy raced through her homework while Crista wasn't even halfway through yet?

Six times seven. Crista certainly knew what six

times five was. Thirty, thirty, thirty. She still remembered how everyone had laughed at her.

Mr. Lopez had said if you couldn't remember how much six times seven was, see if you remembered how much seven times six was, since the answer was the same. Crista looked at her homework and tried to picture seven times six, but nothing came out.

"Chips is the cutest kitten ever!" Jane cried.

"I think he's cuter than Misty," Betsy said. "But don't tell Crista that."

Crista sighed. Lots of times when Betsy didn't want her to know something, she forgot to whisper and Crista found out anyway.

"Misty's cute too," Jane said. "But you're right. Chips is cuter."

Chips was cuter than Misty, Crista thought. But Misty was prettier. And when they were all grown up, it was going to be better for Misty that she was pretty and not cute. When they grew up, Misty was going to be the prettiest cat in the world.

"Oh, look at them!" Jane shouted. "I can't believe they're doing that."

What? Crista wondered. The kittens always seemed to do their cutest stuff when she wasn't around.

"I wish I had a kitten," Jane said. "If I had a kitten, I'd want it to be just like Chips."

That was too much. Nobody was paying attention to poor Misty. The homework would just have to wait.

Crista left her bedroom and went into the living room to see what the kittens were doing. They were curled up next to each other, sleeping.

"They're sleeping?" she asked. "Is that what you were screaming about?"

"We were not screaming," Jane said.

"You should have seen them a minute ago," Betsy said. "Chips was standing up, right on his back legs. He looked so cute. And Misty was running around, and she didn't look where she was going and she ran right into him and knocked him over. It was really funny."

"I bet it was," Crista said. She wished she'd seen it. "Do you think they'll do it again?"

"Maybe," Betsy said.

"No," Jane said. "It was what my mother calls a once-in-a-lifetime experience. She says kittens and babies only do the really best stuff once, and if you don't see it then, you never see it."

"Marty does the same stuff over and over," Crista said.

"Not the same cute stuff," Jane said. "That he only does once. You probably never get to see his cute stuff because you're in school."

"That's right," Betsy said. "I bet we've missed lots of cute stuff."

"And not just Marty's," Jane said. "The kittens', too. I bet they do lots and lots of cute stuff when you're not around."

"They do plenty of cute stuff when we're here," Crista said. "I've seem them do cute stuff."

"I wonder what I've missed," Betsy said. "I bet I've missed practically every cute thing they've ever done."

"Why do you say that?" Crista asked.

"I'm outside more than you are," Betsy said. "Lots of times you'll be sitting around reading and

I'll be outside playing. I bet the kittens do tons of cute stuff when you're reading, and all you have to do is look up and see them. I can't see them from outside."

Jane shook her head. "You've probably missed every cute thing they ever did," she said to Betsy. "Crista's so lucky, getting to see them all the time."

"Crista's the luckiest one," Betsy said. "She's much luckier than I am."

Crista looked at both of them and at the sleeping kittens. If she was so lucky, why did she feel so bad?

Homework Troubles

"**C**ome on, girls," Mr. Linz said that night after supper. "Let me see your homework."

"Here's mine," Grace said.

"Have you been working on your spelling words?" Mr. Linz asked.

Grace nodded. "I'm going to get a hundred next quiz," she said. "I know it."

"Good," her father said. "Betsy, Crista, show me your homework."

"I'm getting it!" Betsy called from their bedroom.

Crista sat at her chair. She'd forgotten all about finishing her homework. She and Betsy and Jane had tried for over an hour to get Chips and Misty to repeat their once-in-a-lifetime experience, but no matter how hard they'd tried, the kittens wouldn't do it. They'd done plenty of other cute things, but Chips didn't stand up and let Misty run into him. And every time the kittens didn't do it, Jane and Betsy would giggle, remembering how cute they'd been.

"Crista, where's your homework?" her father asked.

"I didn't finish it," she said.

"Why not?" her father asked. He didn't sound mad, but Crista knew he was. They were all supposed to do their homework before supper. That was the rule.

"I meant to, but I forgot," Crista said. "I'll finish it now."

"Were you having trouble with it?" her father asked. "Do you want me to help you?"

Crista shook her head. "I just forgot about finishing it," she said. "It won't take long. I'm sorry."

"Let me see it when you're done," her father said.

Crista went into her bedroom. Betsy was just about to walk out with her homework.

"I forgot about finishing," Crista said. "I heard you and Jane talking about the kittens, and I forgot my homework."

"That's terrible," Betsy said. "Can I help?"

"No," Crista said. "I can do it."

She sat alone in the bedroom and tried to remember six times seven. Pretty soon the answer came back to her, and she was able to do all her work.

She showed her father her homework. He didn't scold her, the way she was afraid he would. "Just remember, school is the most important thing," he said. "And doing your homework helps you do better in school."

Crista and Betsy went to bed early that night. The kittens were already asleep, curled up at the foot of Betsy's bed. They'd had a long day too, Crista thought, doing cute things when she wasn't looking.

"Did Daddy get mad at you?" Betsy asked.

"No," Crista said. "He just told me how important homework is."

"That's good," Betsy said. "He got mad at me and I was afraid he'd get mad at you, too."

"Why did he get mad at you?" Crista asked.

"He said it was my fault you hadn't finished," Betsy said. "Because I invited Jane over to play with the kittens. He said it was fine for me to play outside if you weren't through with your homework, but I shouldn't play inside, because then you could hear me and you wouldn't get your work done."

"What did Mommy say?" Crista asked.

"She said we both had to remember that no matter how much we loved the kittens, our schoolwork came first," Betsy said. "I tried to tell them about what Chips and Misty had done, and how we tried to get them to do it again just for you, but they said kittens were going to do cute stuff all the time and we had plenty of chances to see it and I'd better learn to be quiet when you were working. They said you were quiet when I was trying to work and I should do the same for you."

"It's hard to be noisy when you're reading," Crista said.

"I wish you'd remembered to finish your home-work," Betsy said. "That way they wouldn't have scolded me."

"I'm sorry," Crista said. She'd lost track of how often she'd said she was sorry that week, but she knew it wasn't a once-in-a-lifetime experience.

Tooth Troubles

"Ouch!" Crista said the next morning.

"What's the matter?" her mother asked.

"My tooth hurts," Crista said.

"Is it bad?" her mother asked.

Crista nodded. "It started hurting during the night," she said. "And now it's even worse."

Her mother sighed. "Let me call the dentist," she said, "and see when he can see you. You go get dressed."

Crista did. When she came out, her mother had finished on the phone.

"We're seeing him right after school," her mother said.

"But there's a Brownie meeting then," Crista said.

"Sorry," her mother said. "Toothaches come first."

Crista's tooth hurt all during school that day. Her mother sent a note with her so the teachers didn't call on her. That was the only good thing that happened.

After school Crista's mother came to pick her up. Marty was strapped in his car seat in back. Much to Crista's surprise, Betsy joined them.

"Why aren't you going to the Brownie meeting?" Crista asked.

"I have a toothache too," Betsy said. "Ooh, it hurts."

Crista knew that whenever she caught a cold, Betsy got it also. Maybe toothaches were catching too.

"I'll see Crista first," Dr. Thaler said. Crista went into the room and climbed up on the dentist chair. Dr. Thaler asked her which tooth hurt, and Crista showed him. Dr. Thaler poked at the tooth with his instrument, and Crista cried out in pain.

"You have a cavity all right," Dr. Thaler said.

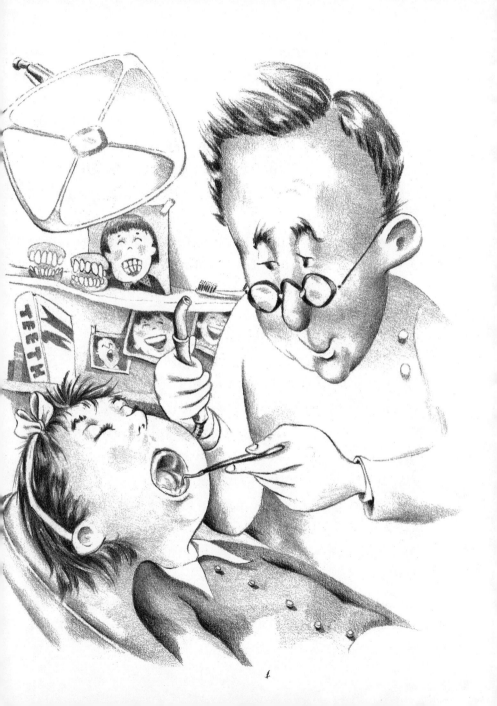

"I'm going to give you a shot of novocaine, Crista. The needle is going to hurt a little bit, but then your tooth will go numb, and you won't feel me drilling. Your mouth will just feel funny for a little while afterward, but there won't be any pain. All right?"

"All right," Crista said. She closed her eyes when Dr. Thaler gave her the shot. It hurt a little more than a little bit, but then there wasn't any pain, and before she knew it, he was all done.

"Betsy's turn," he said.

Crista waited with her mother and Marty. She waited for Marty to do something cute that she wouldn't ordinarily have a chance to see, but Marty only sat in his mother's lap and looked around. Crista wasn't surprised. Nothing was really cute at a dentist's office.

Betsy didn't take nearly as long as Crista. "Twin toothaches," Dr. Thaler said as he brought her out. "There was nothing the matter with Betsy's tooth."

"Then why did it hurt?" Crista asked.

"Because Betsy loves you, I guess," Dr. Thaler

said. "When you don't feel well, she doesn't feel well."

Mrs. Linz paid the dentist and drove them all home. "Crista's homework can wait tonight until after supper," she said. "Let's give the novocaine a chance to wear off. Betsy, why don't you get to work right now."

"All right," Betsy said.

Crista sat in the living room, waiting for the kittens to do something cute. But they were no more in the mood than Marty had been.

Misty was asleep on the sofa. Crista walked over to the sofa and sat down next to Misty. She petted the kitten. Misty purred, but she kept right on sleeping.

Crista picked Misty up. Maybe if she gave her a hug, Misty would wake up and do something cute. Misty purred and snored and never opened her eyes.

"Wake up, stupid," Crista said. She held Misty in her hands and gave her a shake. "Wake up and do something cute for me."

Misty woke up. Her eyes got real big and she

tried to jump out of Crista's grasp. Crista held onto her. Misty wiggled and squirmed, but Crista only held on tighter.

Then Misty scratched Crista's hand and pulled free. "Ouch!" Crista shouted.

Crista's mother came out of the kitchen. "Crista, what's the matter?" she asked.

"Misty scratched me," Crista said. "I was holding on to her and she scratched me."

"You don't need a Band-Aid," her mother said. "But be more careful next time. You can't hold a kitten too hard. They'll fight to get away."

Crista stared at her scratched hand. Her mouth throbbed. Her head hurt. She'd never felt worse in her life.

"Mommy!" she cried, and as soon as her mother was by her side, Crista began to sob.

Digging Up Troubles

"**W**hat's the matter, honey?" her mother asked. "Is it your hand?"

Crista shook her hand. "It's my life," she sobbed. "Everything is awful."

"Oh dear," her mother said. "Tell me about it."

"I wasn't paying attention in arithmetic and I didn't have enough money for my book and the kittens only do cute stuff when I'm not around and I didn't remember to do my homework and I had a toothache and Misty hates me."

"Oh dear, oh dear," her mother said. "It certainly sounds like you've had a terrible week."

"The worst," Crista said.

Crista's mother gave her a kiss. "We all have weeks like that sometimes," she said. "The important thing is to make the bad things stop."

Crista sniffled. "What can I do?" she asked.

"Let me think," her mother said. "Misty will love you again all on her own, you know. And your tooth will stop hurting once the novocaine wears off. And you'll be able to buy the book you want next week."

"Do I have to wait that long?" Crista asked. "I'd like things to get better right away."

"I have an idea," her mother said. "Why don't you go outside and dig a hole?"

"What?" Crista said.

"A hole," her mother said. "I remember my mother once told me to dig a hole and bury all my troubles in it. And you know, I felt a lot better once I did. Get your pail and shovel and dig a nice big hole and throw all the bad things that happened to you this week in it. Then you can throw the dirt over it, and all your troubles will go away."

Crista looked out the window. It was a pretty fall afternoon. The flowers were still blooming and the trees had red and orange leaves. "I'll need to dig a real big hole," she said.

"You can do it," her mother said. "I'll be in the kitchen with Marty and we'll both watch you dig."

Crista wasn't sure it was going to work, but her mother came up with lots of good ideas. She went to her bedroom and looked for her pail and shovel.

"What are you doing?" Betsy asked as Crista dug through their toy chest.

"I need my pail and shovel," Crista said.

"Why?" Betsy asked.

"Mommy told me to dig a hole," Crista said. She found what she was looking for and smiled. "I'll be outside digging," she said. "Bye."

"Bye," Betsy said.

Crista showed her mother the pail and shovel as she walked through the kitchen.

"Dig a nice deep hole," her mother said.

"Ah ah," Marty said.

Crista grabbed her jacket and put it on. She walked around the backyard, looking for the perfect place to dig a hole. Finally she decided on a spot just a few feet away from the kitchen window. That way her mother and Marty could see how well she was doing.

It had rained a few days before, and the ground was still soft. Crista enjoyed digging and making a pile of dirt next to the hole. She didn't use the pail, but she liked having it there by her just in case.

"That's a great hole," Betsy said.

Crista turned around and saw Betsy standing behind her, carrying her own pail and shovel.

"What are you doing?" she asked.

"Mommy said I should dig a hole too," Betsy said. "She said my week was pretty awful too and I'd feel better if I buried my troubles just like you."

"Oh," Crista said.

"I think I'll dig my hole right next to yours," Betsy said. "That way our troubles can keep each other company."

"Okay," Crista said. She started digging again.

Betsy began digging, and she worked very fast. In no time she'd caught up with Crista, and soon her hole was even bigger than her twin's.

"What are you doing?" Crista asked. "You don't need such a big hole."

"Of course I do," Betsy said. "I had a terrible week. Just like you."

"You did not!" Crista said. "I'm the one who had a terrible week."

"I had a worse week," Betsy said.

"Did not!"

"Did too!"

"Did not!" Crista shouted. She started throwing dirt back into her hole, and into Betsy's too, not caring where the dirt landed.

Twin Troubles

"**S**top it!" Betsy said to Crista. "You're burying my troubles too."

"You don't have any troubles," Crista said. "I'm the one who got in trouble at school. I'm the one who didn't do her homework. I'm the one who had the cavity."

"Oh," Betsy said. "I thought I had troubles too."

"You thought you had a toothache," Crista said. "And you didn't."

"But my tooth hurt," Betsy said.

"You didn't have a cavity," Crista said. "You didn't get a shot of novocaine. You didn't have everything go numb."

"No," Betsy said.

"Does your tooth hurt now?" Crista asked.

Betsy felt all her teeth with her tongue. "No," she said. "My tooth stopped hurting when yours did."

"Nothing bad happened to you this week," Crista said. "Everything bad that happened, happened to me."

"Really?" Betsy asked. "It felt like all the bad stuff happened to me too."

Crista shook her head. "Just me, not you," she said.

"Daddy scolded me," Betsy said, "when you didn't do your homework."

Crista thought about it. "Okay," she said. "That was a bad thing that happened to you. But I was the one who forgot about her homework. So it was worse for me. And you got to see the kittens do cute stuff and Misty loves you and not me and I don't care that you didn't get to buy your teddy bear months ago. I didn't get to buy my book this week. I had the worst week of my life this week, and it doesn't make me feel any better when you say your week was even worse."

"I thought it did," Betsy said. "That's why I kept telling you all the bad stuff that happened to me. So you'd feel better."

"It didn't work," Crista said. "It made me sad and then it made me mad, but it never made me feel better."

"Oh," Betsy said. "I want you to feel better. What makes you feel better?"

"Digging a nice big hole," Crista said.

"Could I help you with your hole?" Betsy asked. "Your hole could join mine and then it would be the biggest hole ever. Would that help?"

"You'd give your hole to me?" Crista asked.

"Sure," Betsy said. "I gave my troubles to you."

"Okay," Crista said. "But I want to do all the digging."

"All right," Betsy said. "Can I watch?"

Crista nodded. She picked up her shovel and dug right next to Betsy's hole. It took a minute or two, but then the two holes became one.

"This hole is mine," Crista said. "Just for my troubles."

"Crista's trouble hole," Betsy said. "For burying all your troubles."

Crista threw a shovel's worth of dirt into the hole. "This is for not paying attention in school," she said. "And this is for not having enough money for my book."

"That's a good one," Betsy said. "That was a really good trouble."

"And this is for the kittens doing all their cute stuff when I'm not watching," Crista said. "And this is for forgetting to do my homework." She threw in two more shovels of dirt.

Betsy sat there watching. Crista saw she looked kind of sad.

"I think you should throw some dirt in too," Crista said. "For Daddy scolding you."

"Thank you," Betsy said, and she gave Crista a big smile. "I was hoping you'd let me."

"This is for cavities," Crista said. "Now do one for toothaches."

"This is for toothaches," Betsy said.

"This is for fighting with Betsy," Crista said.

"I'd rather have a hundred toothaches than fight with you," Betsy said.

"I don't think you can have a hundred toothaches," Crista said. "We don't have that many teeth."

"Not even together?" Betsy asked.

Crista shook her head.

"I'd still rather have a lot of toothaches than fight with you," Betsy said.

"Me too," Crista said. "Come on, let's finish with the hole."

The twins filled the big hole with all the dirt they'd dug out. When they finished, they walked into the kitchen together.

"Look at Marty," Betsy said. "He's so cute."

He was, too. He was crawling on the floor trying to pet Chips.

"Meow." Crista looked down and saw Misty standing on her hind legs, trying to climb up Crista's pants. Crista bent down and picked Misty up very carefully. The kitten climbed up her arm, and snuggled on Crista's shoulder. She purred

loudly and licked Crista's cheek.

"She's kissing you," Betsy said. "That is the cutest thing I've ever seen."

"Me too," Crista said. "This is very once-in-a-lifetime."

"The most I've ever seen," Betsy said.

"The most for me, too," Crista said.

"Meow," Misty said, and the twins knew it was the most once-in-a-lifetime experience for her as well.